The Silly Turkey Party

by Steve Metzger
Illustrated by Jim Paillot

SCHOLASTIC INC.

New York Toronto London Auckland Sydney
Mexico City New Delhi Hong Kong Buenos Aires

To Lois, my wonderful sister
—S.M.

To Lisa, Camden, and Rosie
—J.P.

ISBN-13: 978-0-545-06061-5
ISBN-10: 0-545-06061-3

Text copyright © 2008 by Steve Metzger
Illustrations copyright © 2008 by Jim Paillot
All rights reserved. Published by Scholastic Inc.
SCHOLASTIC and associated logos are trademarks
and/or registered trademarks of Scholastic Inc.

12 11 10 9 8 7 6   14 15 16 17/0

Printed in the U.S.A.
First printing, November 2008

Last Thanksgiving Ollie, Cassie, and Wing were heroes.
This year they ruled the roost!

Cassie slept like a princess in a queen-sized bed.

Ollie had his feathers dyed and trimmed.
Wing watched his favorite cartoons in high-definition.

And they all enjoyed Bowling Night with Farmer Joe
and Farmer Kate.
Life was good for Ollie, Cassie, and Wing.

Now, Thanksgiving had arrived again.

Ollie, Cassie, and Wing were relaxing in their hot tub before going to Farmer Joe and Farmer Kate's house for a big holiday dinner.

"I just love the way the bubbles tickle my tail,"
Wing said.

"Gee, I hope my feathers don't get too limp,"
Cassie added. "I want to look my best tonight."

Just then, Farmer Kate appeared.

"Farmer Joe is not feeling well," she announced. "We won't be having Thanksgiving dinner at our home tonight."

The three turkeys listened sadly. "Please try to be quiet," Farmer Kate added as she turned to walk away. "Farmer Joe will be going to bed early. He needs a lot of rest."

As soon as she was out of sight, Ollie spoke up.
"What will we do now?" he asked.
"I guess we're on our own for dinner," Cassie replied.

"Let's invite Pete the Chicken!" Wing declared. "We'll
have a quiet meal of rice and beans...just the four of us."
They raced over to the chicken coop where Pete lived.

"Will you come to our holiday dinner tonight?"
Cassie asked.

"Sure!" Pete replied. "But I thought you were going
to Farmer Joe and Farmer Kate's house."

"Farmer Joe is sick," Wing explained.
"Please don't tell anyone about dinner," Ollie added.
"We need to be quiet so Farmer Joe gets plenty of sleep."
"OK," Pete answered. "Mum's the word."

The three turkeys skipped home as the sun began to set.

Wing swept the floor, Cassie set the table, and Ollie did the cooking.

At 6:00, all was ready. At 6:01, the doorbell rang. "He's a very punctual chicken," Ollie said.

Cassie opened the door and welcomed Pete into their home. But he wasn't alone.

"I hope it's all right," Pete said. "Sally had no place to go for Thanksgiving."

"Uh…sure," Cassie said. "We have enough food.
But you can't make any noise."

They both nodded.

As they ate Ollie's Rice and Beans Delight,
the doorbell rang again.

"Who can that be?" Wing asked,
opening the door. It was the three Duck
sisters—Randy, Sandy, and Mandy!
"What are you doing here?"

"Sally invited us," Mandy replied.

"I'm sorry," Sally said. "They had no place to go."

"We have plenty of food," Wing said. "But you have to be quiet. Farmer Joe is sick."

The Duck sisters nodded as Cassie made room for them at the table.

At first, they were all as quiet as church mice. Then
Sandy told one of her favorite jokes.
"Why did Pete the Chicken cross the road?" she asked.
"Er...I don't know," Cassie replied.

"To play 'Hide and Peep' with Farmer Joe!" Sandy shouted. The Duck sisters laughed so hard they fell off their chairs.

"That quacks me up!" Randy yelled.

"Quiet down," Ollie hissed. "Remember, Farmer Joe is sick."

"Sorry," Mandy whispered. "We'll be quiet."
The doorbell rang again.
"It's getting really crowded in here!" Cassie said
as she hopped over to the door.

Howard the Horse galloped in. "The Duck sisters invited me. But don't worry," Howard said. "I brought enough oats for everyone."

"That was very thoughtful of you," Ollie said. "But you've got to be quiet."

"Sure thing! Sure thing!" Howard whinnied. As he made his way toward the dining room, he knocked over a lamp.

"Oh, my!" Cassie exclaimed. "That will surely wake
up Farmer Joe!"
"So sorry! So sorry!" Howard apologized.

Just then, the doorbell rang again.

"Oh, no!" cried Ollie. "Our home is full! It can't hold anyone else."

When he opened the door, Lulu the Lamb, Shelly the Sheep, and Robbie the Rooster burst in!

"This party needs some energy!" Robbie shouted.
In an instant, Robbie began playing his fiddle, Lulu
banged on a bucket, and Shelly strummed a banjo. Everyone
bounced up and began dancing.

Everyone, that is, except the turkeys.
"Stop! Stop!" Ollie yelled. "You're too loud!"
But the animals were having too much fun to listen.

The three turkeys gave up and sat down.

"Farmer Joe and Farmer Kate will throw us out for sure," Ollie said.

"We might as well pack our bags," Wing added.

DiNG DoNG!

"Not again!" Ollie exclaimed.

It was Farmer Joe and Farmer Kate!

"We're so sorry," Ollie said. "We'll leave in the morning."

"We're not upset," Farmer Kate said. "The music woke up Farmer Joe, and now he's in a terrific mood."

"You said it!" Farmer Joe added. "I feel great!"
"Can we come to your party?" Farmer Kate asked.
"Of course!" Cassie replied.
Farmer Joe and Farmer Kate joined all the animals, dancing late into the night.

As the party drew to a close, Farmer Joe and Farmer Kate walked over to Ollie, Cassie, and Wing.

"We had a wonderful time!" said Farmer Kate.

"Thank you for the best Thanksgiving ever," said Farmer Joe.

The three turkeys were thankful, too. They knew they lived on the best farm in the world!